CHAPTER ONE
Audition!

For perhaps the first time in the school's history, the whole of Year Seven at The Shine School for the Performing Arts had arrived early. They'd been told the day before that there was going to be a mass audition next week for a special Christmas run of *Mary Poppins* at a West End theatre! It was incredibly lucky to get a chance like this in their third week at stage school and all the Year Sevens were desperate to find out more.

Bethany, Chloe and Lily were hanging out by the window in their form room when Sara walked in.

"Wow, you're all early!" she commented.

"So are you!" Bethany pointed out, grinning.

"I couldn't wait to get here," Sara said. "I got the earlier bus! Shove up, then." She dropped her bag and coat on a table and squeezed in next to Lily. "So, has anyone heard any more about the audition?"

"They're coming on Monday," Chloe said shyly. It was only the day before that she'd really made friends with Bethany, Lily and Sara. They hadn't hit it off at the start of term. She and Sara had been sniping at each other for the last three weeks and she was still a bit unsure whether Sara liked her or not.

"Monday! That's not long to get ready. How do you know, Chloe?" Sara leaned eagerly around Bethany. She was an easy-going person and she'd only been so upset with Chloe because she had thought Chloe had been mean to Lily. Sara was very protective of her friends. It had turned out it was all a misunderstanding and now that everything was sorted out, she was happy for them all to hang around together. Besides, even if Chloe was a bit wild sometimes, she had a really cool sense of humour.

"I heard Mr Harvey talking about it as I

came past the staff room this morning." Mr Harvey was their singing teacher. "He was saying the same thing – that he wished he'd had more warning. He'd like to get us to learn a couple of songs, he said."

"Probably most people know them anyway. Everyone knows *Mary Poppins*, don't they?" Sara replied.

"Of course," Bethany agreed. "But do we know them the way Mr Harvey wants us to know them?" She raised one eyebrow at Sara questioningly.

"OK, fair point." Sara sighed and nodded. Three weeks at Shine was quite enough to realize that no one ever knew a song well enough for Mr Harvey. You could do absolutely everything he asked and he would just take it as proof that you were capable of more… Sara adored singing and she couldn't imagine how wonderful it would be to get a part in a West End musical. But so far, all Mr Harvey seemed to have done was criticize her singing. Sara chewed her lip. She might as well face it – she had no chance at the audition if her singing was no good.

"What's the matter?" Bethany asked, spotting her change of mood. "You were over the moon yesterday! I thought being in *Mary Poppins* was your dream come true!"

"You were humming 'A Spoonful of Sugar' all the way down the road," Lily agreed.

Sara shrugged, trying not to look as though it mattered too much. "I know, but what chance have I got? There's all of us and the Year Eights. Yesterday it seemed like fate – my favourite musical and everything. But Mr Harvey doesn't think my singing's any good. There's no way they'll pick me."

Lily made an odd spluttering noise as she spat half her bottle of water down her front in shock at Sara's cluelessness.

"What?" Sara asked, looking confused.

"Mr Harvey thinks you're bound to be a West End princess! You and Bethany are his star pupils! Uuurgh, has anyone got a tissue?"

"He does not! He's always telling me off! Bethany, too," Sara complained. She turned to Bethany for back-up.

"He is, isn't he?"

Bethany nodded gloomily. "I can't do anything right in singing."

Chloe and Lily exchanged disbelieving looks.

"Would you believe anyone could be that dim?" Lily asked, and Chloe shook her head, giggling. "He's always picking on you two because you're so good! He doesn't bother so much with Little Miss Averages like me and Chloe. Haven't you worked that out yet?"

Chloe smiled smugly and tossed her red curls. "It's brilliant. The rest of us go to singing and have a great time, while you two and a couple of others get all the hassle."

Sara wasn't sure whether to be delighted or annoyed. Was Lily right? She glanced at Bethany to see if she agreed and couldn't help smiling. Bethany normally looked so calm and confident but now she looked like someone had just stuffed an ice cube down her back.

"You might have said!" Bethany protested indignantly, and Sara nodded.

"Well, like I told you, I didn't think you

could be stupid enough not to realize!" Lily defended herself, waving the water around dangerously again.

"So if it's singing they're looking for, I reckon you two have got a good chance," Chloe said, seriously now.

Sara glowed. She might have been fighting with Chloe for the past couple of weeks but she did respect her opinion. Was she really that good a singer? It was hard to believe.

"Sara's definitely got more chance than me." Bethany smiled at her. "Sara, tell me you don't already know all the songs from *Mary Poppins* off by heart?"

Sara felt herself go pink. "I just like the songs… I know they're really old, but I love them…"

"Exactly. It's the perfect part for you!"

"You're a better dancer, though," Sara pointed out. "You need to be an all-rounder for something like this, we have to be able to sing, act *and* dance. And you definitely dance better than me."

"Oh, stop it!" Chloe broke in. "You're both brilliant, and you know it. Oh, this is going to be such a fab day. My mum was so excited when I told her we had an audition. She even rang my dad at work to tell him!"

Sara laughed with the others but she couldn't help wishing that her own mum had reacted more like that. She'd gone home buzzing with excitement, and desperate to tell everyone but, as always, her mum only wanted to hear about her academic classes. She was a teacher and was worried that Sara wasn't going to be properly taught at a stage school. It didn't help that Sara's older brother Will had just got brilliant grades in his GCSEs. Her parents were always comparing the two of them and Sara couldn't get them to see that she was a totally different sort of person. Sometimes she felt like she must have been swapped at birth, and somewhere a really brainy eleven-year-old was trying to convince her parents that she hated dancing...

Luckily, Sara's gran shared her passion for show business and had always been really supportive. It had been her gran sitting in the front row at all her dance school shows when her mum and her dad had had work stuff to go to. And it was Gran who'd persuaded them to let Sara try out for Shine. Sara suspected that they'd never thought she'd get in, so they hadn't worried too much about it.

When the letter arrived saying she'd got a place, there had been a huge row. Sara shuddered just remembering it. The letter had come addressed to her, although there was loads of stuff in it for her parents, too. She saw the big Shine logo on the envelope as Will handed it to her at breakfast and she knew at once what it was. She sat paralyzed, not wanting to open it. What if she hadn't got a place? She'd been telling herself for weeks that it was very unlikely she would. After all, about two hundred people had auditioned for thirty places, so she didn't have much of a chance. It was better to assume she wouldn't get in and then she wouldn't be so disappointed. That was the plan, anyway.

Her parents had kept on talking about Sara going to Meadow Park, the local school that her mum taught at and where Will was doing so well. Every time they mentioned it Sara had felt worse and worse. It was like they just assumed she didn't have a hope of getting into Shine, either. Somehow it was OK for her to tell herself that, but a bit of encouragement from her parents would have been nice!

"What's that, Sara? Something from the writers' club?" Her mum had bought her membership in a young writers' club for her birthday, despite the hints Sara had dropped about new tap shoes.

"It's from the school," Sara murmured, staring at the words on the envelope – *The Shine School for the Performing Arts*.

"What? From Meadow Park? Why on earth are they writing to you? I didn't know anything about a mailing going out to new students." Her mum reached across the table to take the envelope. "Let me see."

"No! It's addressed to me and it's not from Meadow Park, it's from Shine." Sara snatched the envelope into her lap, glaring at her mother.

"Oh. That." Her mother sighed and exchanged a glance with her father. "Well, aren't you going to open it?"

If only the post arrived a little bit later, Sara thought miserably. She really didn't want to read the letter with Mum, Dad and Will all staring at her. It would be bad enough knowing that she had to go to Meadow Park and spend years with all the staff telling her what a pleasure Will had been to teach and everyone else hating her because her mum was a teacher.

She poked her nail into the corner of the envelope and slowly tore it open across the top. It was quite fat and a couple of leaflets fell out as she opened it. She didn't see her mum's face changing as she watched. Sara's mum knew enough about schools to realize that this wasn't a "no".

Sara picked up the white sheet with the embossed red letterhead and scanned it, slowly at first, then faster and faster as she tried to take in what it was saying.

We are delighted to offer you a place in Year Seven, commencing this September…

"I got in!" she whispered, still staring at the letter in her hand. Then she looked up delightedly and shrieked, "I got in! I can go to Shine!" She shoved back her chair and started dancing round the table waving the letter, while her parents sat stunned.

Sara stuffed the letter into her mother's hand and grabbed Dusty the cat to have someone to dance with.

"Read it! Isn't it brilliant? I've got a place!"

"That's really great, Sara. Well done!" Will was beaming at her. They might not have much in common – especially as he was five years older than her – but they got on pretty well.

"Sara, slow down," her mother murmured.

"Dusty doesn't mind! He likes dancing, don't you, Dusty? I'll be teaching him jazz and modern now – they do both at Shine." Sara twirled round, the cat gazing with resignation over her shoulder.

"That's not what I meant." Her mum sighed. "Just because you've got a place, it doesn't necessarily mean—"

Sara stopped mid-twirl and the cat gave a little mew of relief. "What?" she asked breathlessly. "What are you talking about?"

Her mum gave her dad a 'Help me!' look. He was pretending to read his post very carefully and was obviously trying not to get involved. "Gavin!" she snapped, and he laid the letters down reluctantly.

"Sara, that school is very expensive. The fees are enormous." Her father looked at her apologetically.

"We can't afford it?" Sara's voice was almost a whimper and her eyes were filling with tears.

"Well, not easily—"

"You said if I got into Queen Charlotte's, that you'd do anything to find the fees. I heard you. Why can't you do that for Shine?"

Sara's mum gave a dismissive snort. "That's totally different, Sara. Queen Charlotte's is one of the best girls' schools in the area. Obviously if you'd got in there—"

"But I didn't! I got into one of the best theatre schools in the *country* and you're not even pleased for me! You haven't even said 'Well done!'"

"Darling, of course we're pleased…" Her dad was looking upset and Sara noticed Will making a quick getaway, casting her an apologetic look as he gathered up his school stuff.

"We don't really want you to go to a theatre school," her mother said through gritted teeth.

"Then why did you let me audition?" Sara wailed. "Because you thought I was useless and I'd never get a place! That's it, isn't it? I didn't get into stupid Queen Charlotte's and you can't boast about how clever I am to all your friends like you do with Will, so you just think I'm no good at anything!"

"This has nothing to do with Will or how clever you are!" Her mum was getting really angry now. "I don't agree with specialist schools like Shine and I don't want you turning into some horrible little child star who shows off all the time. You won't get a properly rounded education at a school like that."

Sara sniffed back her tears and prepared to do battle. "It says in the prospectus that Shine is at the top of the local league table for exam results. You might know that if you'd ever bothered to look at it!"

"Sara, I am not having this argument with you now. I'm very pleased that you've got a place but you're hardly behaving in a way that's going to encourage us to support you—"

"Because you're saying I can't go! How do you expect me to behave?" Sara put the cat down on the table and grabbed her rucksack. "I hate you!" she hissed as she stalked past her mother. It was childish but she couldn't think of anything better. And anyway, just then, she really did.

"What are you looking like that for?" Lily nudged her. "Are you panicking about the audition? I've never seen you look so miserable!"

Sara laughed and tried to shrug it off. "Just daydreaming," she said, but the other three didn't look convinced.

"You're not that good an actress – yet," Bethany said, grinning. "What's wrong?" Then she added hurriedly, "I mean, you don't have to say if it's private or anything!"

"No, it's OK," Sara said. She felt it might help to tell them. After all, these were her friends.

"I was just wishing my parents were more excited about the audition. My mum hardly even listened when I told her about it." Sara tried to sound as though she didn't care but the shocked looks on the others' faces made it hard.

"She's – she's a teacher and she's just not into that sort of thing," she muttered. It felt so awful admitting that her mum wasn't interested. "My parents didn't really want me to come here. My gran had to persuade them. She's paying half my fees as well. But if I don't get a really good report in all my classwork at the end of term, I have to go to a normal school."

"Wow," Chloe said. "No wonder you weren't keen on me messing around in class."

Bethany looked totally disbelieving. "How can they not be proud of you for getting in here? It's one of the best schools ever. I mean, that sounds like I'm boasting but we're so lucky! Don't they get that?"

"They want me to be a genius like my brother," Sara said sadly. "I'm really not."

Lily put an arm round her shoulders. "Yeah, you don't need to tell us that. We heard what Miss James said about your maths homework."

Sara chuckled, feeling a little bit better. "Mmm."

"When my brother was in Year Seven, the school had to get him a different maths textbook because he'd done everything in the normal one in about a week."

"Bet he can't sing though," Chloe put in, leaning round to look at her.

"Our cat's better," Sara agreed, thinking of Will humming tunelessly along to his music while he worked.

"So if the rest of your family don't do anything like singing or dancing, where do you get it from?" Bethany asked curiously. "I mean, my mum's never done anything professional but she sings all the time. And my sister's in this really great band at school."

"My gran used to be a dancer," Sara explained. "She's my mum's mum. My grandad fell in love with her when he saw her on stage. He sent her flowers to the stage door for weeks. Gran hoped Mum would want to dance but she never liked it much. So she was really pleased when I took to it. My parents used to say she was just encouraging me to show off, but it was Gran who took me to dancing and she arranged for me to come and audition here. My mum reckoned that she wanted me to be her all over again but that's just not true," she added quickly. "Gran was even happier when it turned out I was a good singer because that was different to her. She got a friend of hers to teach me, someone she knew from her time in the theatre."

"Well, when you get the part in *Mary Poppins*, your mum and dad will have to admit you're a star," Chloe said firmly. "We're all going to kill ourselves trying on Monday, don't get me wrong, but I reckon you're bound to get a callback. Then they'll see."

Sara nodded, forcing herself to smile. She hoped so, too. This was her big chance to prove herself to her parents but she had a horrible suspicion that a part in a West End show wasn't going to be her parents' dream come true...

CHAPTER TWO
Sara's Chance to Shine

At morning break Sara and the others headed to the cafeteria. Sara usually enjoyed science classes, but she'd spent the double lesson obsessing about the audition, and so had the others. They needed sugar.

"I swear, she could make how to – I don't know – explode a *frog* boring," moaned Chloe, who really didn't like Mrs Taylor. "Do you think it's something teachers have special lessons in?"

"No one could be that dull without some

kind of training," Bethany agreed. "Do I want a cereal bar or a muffin?" The Shine cafeteria was very healthy and an oatmeal-raisin muffin was about as close to a treat as you could get. "It's history next, isn't it? Definitely the muffin, then."

They sat down at one of the tables and the conversation went back to the audition. It was all anyone could think about.

"Do you think the casting team will see our year separately or will it be us and the Year Eights together?" Sara wondered.

"Talking of Year Eights, look what just crawled in." Chloe's voice dripped with disgust. "*Lizabeth*."

True enough, the tall blonde girl was walking over to the next table. Lizabeth would have been very pretty indeed if she didn't always look as though she'd just smelled something horrible. She was with a small group of Year Eight girls, who all carefully cultivated the same sneering expression and agreed with every word Lizabeth said.

Lily pretended to be focused on opening her cereal bar. She couldn't stand Lizabeth. On their first day at Shine, Lizabeth and her gang had really picked on Lily and now she stayed out of their way as much as she could.

"Of course," Lizabeth said airily as she sank gracefully into a seat, "I'm bound to get a callback." The rest of her group nodded wisely. "I mean, I look perfect for the part and Mr

Harvey thinks my voice is truly special. He said so."

Unfortunately, Bethany couldn't hold back a disbelieving snort. Unless Mr Harvey had a personality transplant when he taught Year Eight, there was no way he had said anything like that. He was more likely to tell Lizabeth that she sounded like a bloodhound with flu, which is exactly what he'd said to Carmen, one of the twins in Year Seven, on Monday. And he'd said her sister, Ella, was worse. The twins hadn't minded that much but they'd mouthed their way through the rest of the lesson.

Lizabeth swung round, her eyes narrowing. She looked like a snake homing in on prey with a whole nest of little snake mates to back her up.

Bethany swallowed her mouthful of muffin nervously. She wasn't as scared of Lizabeth as Lily was, but no one really wanted to get on the wrong side of her. Too late now, though.

"You lot," Lizabeth snarled. "Little Miss Ferrars and her bunch of loser friends. I might have known." She turned back to her table, smirking. "Can you believe that the school are actually letting this lot audition for *Mary Poppins* with us? Ms Purcell must be off her head."

Lizabeth's 'best friend' Nadia, who was really just the girl who sucked up to her most, giggled infuriatingly. "I should think it's to give us something to look good against. There's no way anyone would actually cast *them* in a West End show."

Sara stamped on Chloe's foot. Chloe had a temper that was as fiery as her red hair and she was obviously about to go ballistic. But she hadn't noticed that Lily had gone two shades paler than normal and was looking as though she was about to throw up.

"Leave it!" Sara muttered as Chloe blinked at her. She threw a meaningful glance sideways at Lily and Chloe got the point. With as much dignity as possible, they got up and stalked out of the cafeteria, Chloe scowling back at Lizabeth and her sniggering group.

"If she gets a callback, I'm going to murder her first," Chloe muttered as they headed back to their form room.

"The problem is, when she turns on the charm she's like the world's sweetest person," Sara said gloomily. "And she does look just right for Jane Banks, if they're going by the way the children look in the film." Sara loved

the original film of *Mary Poppins* – it was
full of amazing songs. It was Mary Poppins
herself, the children's nanny, who had most of
the best bits. Jane and Michael Banks were the
children she was looking after, and they got to
sing quite a lot, too.

"Yeah, you and Lizabeth actually look really
alike," Bethany said, giggling. She nudged Lily
encouragingly. "Don't they?"

"Ugh, we do not." Sara made sick noises.

Lily managed a feeble smile and the others
looked at her sympathetically. Lizabeth had
really got to her.

In singing that afternoon, Mr Harvey was in
full *Mary Poppins* mode, getting them to work
on 'A Spoonful of Sugar'. He said it was what
they would have to sing for the audition on
Monday, so everyone was trying really hard.

Sara was enjoying herself and it was a song she loved. For once, Mr Harvey wasn't picking her up on every little thing. Maybe he was trying not to stress them out before the audition, she thought. Her only problem was that it made her want to dance as well! She couldn't stop bouncing in her seat and when they put down their music to stand round the piano, she just couldn't resist a little twirl at the end. She went scarlet when she realized it hadn't been an imaginary twirl, but everyone laughed, even Mr Harvey.

"Nice to see someone enjoying themselves," he commented. "Remember that when you enjoy a song, it shows in your singing. That's why I want you all to know this song backwards. Then you can just relax and enjoy it on Monday."

Sara exchanged disbelieving glances with the others. OK, so she was enjoying the song now but she couldn't imagine being relaxed enough to enjoy *any* of Monday. She was going to be terrified!

In tap on Thursday afternoon, Ms Driver spent the lesson preparing them for the audition, too. It was going to be a bit like their audition for Shine, where everyone had to dance along with the teacher. No one would be doing special audition pieces, not yet anyway. The casting team from the theatre would teach them a short routine and see how they picked it up. So Ms Driver was giving them a practice

go, demonstrating a simple sequence of steps
a couple of times and getting them to repeat it
back.

"Remember this is a performance, girls!
You're out to impress! Smile and try to look as
though you're having fun!"

Sara realized that she had been scowling
in an effort to keep the routine in her head.
It was so difficult to remember what to do
and remember to smile! It was no good just
sticking a fixed grin on your face – it had to
be a real, relaxed smile. Sara smiled to herself
as she remembered her friend Lulu in her
old dance school's Christmas show. Lulu
was meant to be a snow fairy, but Sara's gran
said afterwards that she looked more like a
toothpaste ad!

"Lovely, Sara! Keep that nice smile! And
shuffle, hop, step!" Ms Driver sounded
approving and Sara couldn't hold back a huge

beam. Maybe she should try and remember Lulu on Monday…

Everyone was so focused on Monday's audition that the time seemed to fly by. Sara spent quite a lot of the weekend holed up in her bedroom watching the old *Mary Poppins* film, trying to sing and dance along. She kept crashing into her bookcase though, and on Sunday afternoon Will came in, looking irritable.

"Are you *still* watching that? I can hear it through the wall, you know. Aren't you sick of it yet? Those chimney sweeps are driving me mad!"

Sara pressed pause and gave him an apologetic look. "Sorry. It's just that the audition's tomorrow and I can't think about anything else!"

Will looked confused. "What audition? You didn't say you had one. That's really cool!"

"Oh, I'm sorry, I forgot. All of our class get to try out for *Mary Poppins*. It's going to be at the Theatre Royal over Christmas! I told Mum but she wasn't really interested, so…"

Will nodded. "Mmm. I get it. Bet Gran was over the moon though."

Sara grinned. "Yeah, I watched the film at hers yesterday, too. We both danced!"

"Well, all right then. I don't mind listening

to that idiot trying to do a cockney accent if it's for a good reason." He headed back to try and finish his homework, and Sara started the video again, lying flat on her bed and kicking in time to the music. If she half-closed her eyes, she could almost see herself dancing along with Julie Andrews and the cartoon penguins…

The audition was being held instead of tap and singing on Monday afternoon, and no one could concentrate at all that morning. In geography, Chloe's friend Sam wasn't paying attention and quite seriously told Mrs Carrington that volcanoes were like chimneys. Everyone roared with laughter. It wasn't really that funny but they were all keyed up and needed to laugh. Mrs Carrington looked a bit confused but beamed at Sam and said it was actually a very clever way of putting it. He looked smug for the rest of the morning.

At lunchtime, the cafeteria was buzzing. It was only the Year Sevens and Eights who were auditioning but the whole school was excited. Sara, Lily, Bethany and Chloe squeezed round one long table with Sam and a couple of the other boys, and the twins, Carmen and Ella.

"It's so weird…" Sara muttered, picking at her baked potato. She was way too excited to actually eat it.

The others waited for a minute, then Bethany asked patiently, "What is?"

"Oh! Sorry, I was thinking aloud. It's weird to be auditioning all of us together. I mean, don't get me wrong, I wouldn't want to be doing it on my own! But don't you think it's funny that we're all trying out for the same thing? And only one of us can get it?"

The others nodded thoughtfully. "Just think

what it's like trying out against your own twin!" Carmen said, and Ella made a face.

"Yeah, that must be awful!" Sara gazed at them wide-eyed. "I hadn't even thought of that."

"It's just one of those things," Ella shrugged. "We all have to get used to it, I guess."

"Hey, we've only got ten minutes till the end of lunch," Chloe gasped. "We'd better go and change."

The casting team were going to see the girls dancing first, so they needed their footless tights and the Shine T-shirts they wore for tap classes. They had to bring jazz shoes as well as tap shoes because there wasn't going to be much actual tap in the production they were auditioning for. And for once, they didn't have to have their hair tied back. Ms Driver had explained that the casting team wanted to see them with their hair down. Sara had spent ages putting intensive conditioner on hers the night before, so long that her mum had asked her if she was moving into the bathroom permanently. But hopefully it might just help!

"I feel all wrong with my hair loose for a dance class!" Chloe giggled as she brushed hers out. "I keep panicking that someone's going to tell me off." At the beginning of term, Chloe had got into trouble with Ms Driver over not doing her hair properly for tap.

"If that's all you're panicking about, think yourself lucky," muttered Sara, twisting to see herself in the mirror. The changing rooms were crowded, with all the Year Seven and Eight girls trying to look their best.

Chloe looked back over her shoulder. "Hey! You're not seriously nervous, are you? You've got such a good chance at this, Sara, honestly. You mustn't let nerves spoil it."

"It's easy to say that, Chloe! Don't you *ever* get nervous?" she asked curiously, twisting a strand of hair round her finger.

"Course I do. Everyone does! But what do you normally do for nerves? What about when you have dance exams and stuff?"

Sara shrugged. "I don't know. I don't think dance exams are that scary, somehow. An audition's different." She shuddered, remembering. "I was terrified all through the audition to get in here. I was nearly sick in between the ballet and tap."

Lily gave her an amazed look. "Were you

really? I remember seeing you at the audition, and I thought you looked fantastic. So calm!"

Bethany looked up from the bench, where she was putting on her tap shoes. "You're all going to kill me for saying this but it's not all that important, you know! It's our first audition here – so what if it's not perfect? We're going to have hundreds of them!"

Sara, Lily and Chloe gazed at her in amazement, but then they looked at each other and shrugged. Bethany was right. Going into the audition stressed out would be a disaster.

"So you're saying just relax and enjoy it?" Sara asked Bethany, making a face. "That's what my mum said about my SATs. She really thought I'd enjoy them if I just tried hard enough…" She giggled, and then took a deep breath, uncurling her spine slowly. It was a great relaxation exercise her gran had shown her. Right. Enjoy it…

"Hi everyone! I'm Tamara. I'm an assistant choreographer for the show. I'm just going to go through a few steps for you and then we'll get small groups to dance them. OK?"

Tamara seemed really nice but it was hard to ignore the other people from the theatre, all clutching notebooks. Sara and the others watched carefully as Tamara danced, explaining as she went. It was a simple routine, Sara noted gratefully. She saw Carmen and Ella making faces at each other – the twins had only just started tap and obviously Tamara's moves looked a bit scary.

"Everyone got that?"

As if we'd dare say no! Sara thought and grinned to herself. Chloe and Bethany were right – the only way to do this was to try and enjoy it. She just hoped she'd be in the first group to go. She wasn't sure she could stand waiting much longer.

Luckily she was standing near the front and Tamara picked the first five girls she could see – Sara, Chloe and three Year Eight girls they didn't know. It felt so lonely, out in the middle of the huge studio.

Sara glanced back to Bethany and Lily, who were making thumbs-up signs at her and flashed a quick smile at them. Out of the corner of her eye, she spotted Lizabeth, looking contemptuous. The older girl was swishing her long blond hair about, trying to catch the attention of the casting team.

A grim determination took over inside Sara. Lizabeth obviously wasn't nervous. She looked as though she was having the time of her life. Sara knew she was a pretty good dancer. She wasn't as brilliant as some of her class but there was no way she was going to let Lizabeth do better than her. The thought of how furious the snotty Year Eight would be if she, Sara, got a callback made a natural smile the easiest thing in the world.

As the music started, Sara's nerves melted away and it was one of those fantastic moments where the steps just seemed to flow. Sara found herself in the final floor pose without quite knowing how she'd got there and heard a storm of clapping.

"Well done, girls!" Was it Sara's imagination or was Tamara smiling especially at her? She headed back to the others, breathing fast, and saw Lizabeth eyeing her. She definitely didn't look happy and that made Sara feel even better.

"You were fantastic!" Bethany handed Sara her fleece. "That's easily the best I've seen you dance *and* you had to do it first time."

Sara glowed. Bethany and Chloe were tap stars, so if Bethany thought she'd done well, it had to mean something. She turned to give Chloe a quick hug. "We did it!" she whispered.

"It was cool!" Chloe was bouncing on her toes with excitement. "Even if I don't get a callback, that was so fun. And you were amazing. I saw you do that difficult leg swap thing – what did she call it? Oh, I can't remember, but you had it perfectly. I thought I was going to fall over!"

The buzz from the dance audition carried Sara through the singing. They were in little groups again but this time the musical director, Simon, did get some people to sing a few phrases solo. Sara was pretty sure by her turn that he was only getting the best people to sing alone. She was so glad they'd practised 'A Spoonful of Sugar'! But in a way that actually made it harder, because Simon seemed to want different intonations from Mr Harvey and the stress on different words. Not everyone was picking up on that.

"Right – last group!"

Sara came up to the piano with Bethany, Carmen, Ella, Chloe and Lily. She could feel Lizabeth's eyes drilling into her back, willing her to mess up. She'd been death-staring her all the way through the audition. Obviously she'd decided that Sara was competition, despite what she'd said about Year Sevens being useless. But Sara wasn't freaked. Lizabeth was scary but she couldn't do anything in the middle of the audition! And knowing that someone else thought she was doing well just made Sara glow inside. She beamed at Simon and he smiled back.

"OK, you've probably heard this way too many times already but I'll play it through for you again." He was already starting on the intro. Sara followed along, tapping her foot gently without even realizing she was doing it. She *so* wanted to sing! "Now you. Intro again, and you come in after three. One, two, three, and…"

At last! Sara sang out happily, trying hard to put the words across the way he'd shown them. She could hear Bethany's bell-like voice supporting her, and the others in the background.

"That was nice. Very nice." Simon looked carefully at each of them, scribbling some notes. "I'd just like to hear a couple of you again, to make sure… Would you sing the first few lines again for me – Bethany, is it?" He peered at the sticky label on her T-shirt. Bethany blushed delightedly and nodded. "Off we go then."

Wow. Bethany's voice was just so good – so clear and she hit the high notes with no effort whatsoever. Sara had always hoped she was good but she was pretty sure Bethany was better. Still, she thought there were a few times when Bethany could have placed her words better. She was hoping that Simon would ask her to sing alone, too.

"Lovely. And Sara." He grinned at her, obviously seeing how keen she was. "Could you do those lines, too?"

Sara nodded excitedly. Now she had her

chance, she must *not* mess this up! It would
be easy to get overconfident, having heard the
song so many times already. Simon's hands
flashed over the keys and he nodded her in.

Sara sang her way through the chorus,
loving the chance to perform, her nerves
completely gone. As she reached the last line,
she took a breath, eager to go on to the verse,
and Simon grinned and
kept playing for her.
She sang for longer
than any of the
others and she could
feel people were
enjoying it. The
casting team were
smiling as she
finally stopped
after the second
chorus.

"Very nice," was all Simon said, but she could feel the warmth in his voice. "Thank you, Sara." He made a few more notes and then looked round at all the girls. "Thanks so much, everybody. We'll be in touch with a callback list, hopefully tomorrow, and we'll aim for callbacks this time next week."

He gave Sara one last grin and she followed the others out of the classroom, feeling as though she were floating. She'd done it – her first show audition!

CHAPTER THREE
The Shortlist

Sara and the others streamed out into the corridor on a wave of excitement. Everyone felt they'd done reasonably well but it was obvious to the others that Sara had really shone. Sara was torn between wanting to jump up and down and being desperate not to gloat! So she wandered happily along to the changing room, surrounded by the chattering group.

Suddenly an angry voice stopped them in

their tracks. "There you are!" Of course, it was Lizabeth. Sara, who'd been daydreaming that she was already on the Theatre Royal stage, gaped as Lizabeth thrust a finger in her face. "Just what did you think you were doing in there?" she snapped. "That audition was for our year. You lot were just there to fill up the numbers. You shouldn't have been showing off like that. You've totally embarrassed yourself and the school! You should be really ashamed."

Sara stared back at her in horror. Was Lizabeth right?

She'd really thought that her singing went well, but what if the casting team were just being nice and not wanting to upset her? Stricken, she glanced round at Bethany, Lily and Chloe. Did *they* think she'd just made a massive fool of herself?

Bethany folded her arms and glared at the older girl. She had been watching Lizabeth's calculated effort to ruin Sara's emotional high. She was quite a bit shorter than Lizabeth but she was still squaring up to her. "Didn't like the competition, huh? I notice you only got to sing two lines solo. Was that because Simon could see how perfect your voice was after the first note? Or perhaps he just couldn't stand any more?"

"Yeah, right!" Lizabeth looked stunned that a Year Seven was daring to stand up to her. It seemed to have robbed her of any good comebacks. She was about to get an even bigger shock – Lily was wading in.

"How dare you say that to Sara? She was fantastic and you know it! You're just jealous!" Lily spat angrily.

If Lizabeth was shocked, it was nothing to how Sara and the others felt. Lizabeth scared Lily so much that normally she turned into jelly whenever she saw her Year Eight gang. What on earth had come over their friend? Lily looked surprised at herself as well, but quietly pleased at the same time. Lizabeth looked like she was either going to explode or faint.

Chloe decided that enough was enough. She shoved the others on down the corridor, turning back to wave and call, "Bye, Lizabeth! I'd shut your mouth if I were you. You look like a goldfish and you wouldn't want the casting team to see you like that!" Then she ran.

Back in the changing room, Sara was sitting on one of the benches, looking dazed. "I can't believe you lot just stuck up for me like that," she muttered at last.

"She had it coming," said Bethany firmly.

"Yeah, but it's Lizabeth! We're dead. And you, Lily. What came over you? When she was a having a go at you at lunch last week, you looked like you were going to pass out! And then you go and yell at her!"

Lily shrugged. "I don't know. I guess she

just went too far this time. I mean, you were fantastic. You do know that, don't you? I couldn't bear watching her trying to spoil it for you. It was just … wrong."

Sara flushed pink. "We all did well," she said firmly. "We don't know what'll happen or what they were really looking for. And the girl and the boy will have to look right together, so that might change who they go for. Any of us might get a callback."

The others exchanged glances. OK, so Sara didn't want them going on about it, but they were all certain the casting team had loved her.

All the next morning, the school's main corridor seemed to be full of Year Sevens and Eights. They were haunting the notice boards, just in case the callback list went up. Every time a member of staff walked past and looked as though they might have a piece of paper in their hand, the whole group held its breath.

At the beginning of break, Sara, Lily, Bethany and Chloe sped down to the corridor to join them.

"How did everyone get here so quickly?" Chloe asked, looking at the heaving mass. "I mean, we ran as quickly as we could."

"No idea." Bethany shook her head. "Oh, look! There's Mr Lessing!"

The drama teacher was walking past, smiling to himself. Everyone tensed up, especially when Mr Lessing pulled a piece of paper out of the folder he was carrying. He seemed to be reading it as he walked along. Everyone craned their necks to see, and when he sidestepped a few Year Eights to get closer to the notice boards, a huge gasp went up. This was it!

Then he walked straight past! He happened

to catch Sara's eye as he went and winked at her. Sara exchanged a long-suffering look with the others. "I bet he did that on purpose," she said, shaking her head. "He was teasing us all! Well, I think it's stupid waiting around here. We're not exactly *not* going to know if the list goes up. The news will be round the school in seconds! Let's go and get a drink." She marched off, determined not to let the suspense get to her.

Bethany, Lily and Chloe nodded. Chloe felt like staying, but not on her own. She gave one last hopeful look around for approaching teachers, then followed her friends.

It was a cold day and the cafeteria was deliciously warm – and nearly empty. Sara and the others gathered round one of the prime window tables and sipped their tea. Sam from their year was there with a couple of his mates and they crowded round the table, too.

"Thought you lot would be hovering by the notice boards," Sam said curiously.

"Couldn't be bothered." Sara grinned at him. "You don't fancy yourself in *Mary Poppins*, then?"

"Nah." Tom and Jake snorted disbelievingly and Sam looked a bit sheepish. "Well, OK, I wouldn't say no, exactly… But there didn't seem much point hanging around looking desperate."

"Exactly." Bethany nodded.

"Hear you got on the wrong side of Lizabeth at the audition," Jake said slyly.

Sara shook her head in amazement. "Nothing happens in this place without everyone else knowing about it in minutes."

"Who isn't on the wrong side of Lizabeth, any—"

Chloe was suddenly cut off by a double whirlwind appearing next to the table and grabbing Sara. "Come on! Come and see!" The twins were practically dragging her out of her seat, but Sara sat like a statue. "Come on, you muppet! You have to come and read the list. It's up!" Carmen said impatiently.

Surely Carmen and Ella wouldn't be doing this if she wasn't on the list, Sara thought. They wouldn't be so mean. She stood up slowly, feeling as though her stomach had dropped to her toes. The others were dashing off, even the boys, but Bethany came back to link arms with her. "Hey! Aren't you excited?" she asked.

"Yeah," Sara admitted. "Course I am. I'm just a bit – I just feel a bit funny. I don't know why."

"Well, I'd be over the moon," Bethany said, "but it's a big thing. I can see why you might feel weird. Don't you want to look at the list?"

Suddenly Sara found that she did, very much. "Of course I do!" she yelped and grabbed Bethany's hand, racing her down the stairs. They elbowed their way to the front of the crowd and found Carmen, Ella, Lily and Chloe right by the list.

"Look!" Chloe squeaked, jabbing her finger at the piece of paper headed with the Theatre Royal logo. "That's you!" She hugged Sara tightly. "You did it!" Chloe was right. Sara peered over her shoulder and the list definitely did say *Sara Sinclair*. There were five girls' names, and five boys' underneath.

"Who are the others?" Sara murmured, trying to see. Lily, Chloe and the twins exchanged glances.

"Well, they're all Year Eights. You're the only Year Seven who got a callback, girls *and* boys. That's really impressive," said Lily reassuringly.

"OK. What aren't you telling me?" Sara folded her arms. "Oh, no! She didn't, did she?"

Lily nodded, looking almost apologetic. "And one of the others is her mate Nadia. I don't know how they did it, the casting team must have had a moment of madness or something."

Yes, right underneath *Sara Sinclair* was *Lizabeth Mackenzie*. Sara was up against Lizabeth for a part that she had a feeling the Year Eight girl would do anything to get.

Sara had to really force herself to concentrate for the rest of the morning. All she wanted to think about was the audition – how excited she was and how much she wished Lizabeth wasn't doing it, too. Still, she was determined that Lizabeth wasn't going to spoil it for her. She deserved this and no one could take that away.

Doodling happily in her book during maths, she happened to look up and see Chloe, sitting on the other side of their table. Chloe had her chin on her hand and was gazing miserably down at her textbook. She was too far away for Sara to whisper to her and it didn't seem fair to pass a "What's up?" message all the way round the table. What if Chloe didn't want everyone fussing?

Suddenly a horrible thought struck Sara. Was Chloe miserable because she hadn't got a callback? Sara hadn't really considered how her friends must be feeling right now. They'd all been so lovely, almost more excited than she was about her triumph, but what if deep down they were disappointed or even jealous? Chloe certainly didn't look happy.

Sara did a quick scan round the rest of the table. None of the others seemed down. Carmen and Ella were giggling over something together, Bethany was working and Lily was looking at the whiteboard.

Sara suddenly remembered that their homework was to do the maths problems they didn't finish in class and gave one last look at Chloe. There was nothing she could do right now, so she went back to her worksheet. It didn't seem to be making much sense... She sighed. She'd have to ask Will to explain to her at home. Right now she was more worried about Chloe than she was about triangles. She was going to try and grab her friend after the lesson and find out what was the matter.

Chloe still didn't seem her usual self at lunch, Sara thought. She was definitely quiet – and that just wasn't Chloe. Sara nudged herself into a seat next to Chloe's at the lunch table and hoped that the others would find some juicy gossip so she could have a quiet word. Unfortunately the juicy gossip was her and the callback audition.

"Has anyone said what you need to do for Monday, Sara?" Carmen asked eagerly.

"Carmen! When exactly has Sara not been in the same room as you since break?" Bethany asked, shaking her head. "How could anyone have told her? Or do you reckon that now she's up for a part she's got some sort of radio link-up with Ms Purcell?"

Carmen and the others laughed at the thought of their deeply scary principal sending Sara secret messages.

"You will be at the drama studio wearing a frog costume…" intoned Lily, doing a worryingly good impression of Ms Purcell's perfect diction.

Sara couldn't help laughing, too, but she was super-sensitive right now and worried that Bethany's silly comment was hiding something. She just couldn't hold it back any longer. "Do you mind about it?" she blurted out.

Everyone looked at her, confused. "Mind

about what?" Bethany asked eventually.

"A-about the callback…" Sara explained, stammering a little.

Carmen leaned towards her. "You mean, are we jealous?"

Sara nodded unhappily, but Carmen's response was totally unexpected. She burst out laughing and Ella answered for her. "Of course we are!"

Chloe said, in a very serious voice, "We're all considering poisoning you and going in your place on Monday." She rolled her eyes. "Don't be stupid, Sara, we're as jealous as anything! But it doesn't mean we're upset with *you*."

"Just the stupid, bad-taste casting team," said Bethany, grinning. "I reckon Lizabeth got my place and I'm never forgiving them. But seriously, Sara, I knew I wouldn't get a callback. I totally messed up in the dance audition."

"It didn't look like it to me," Sara said, surprised.

"That's because you were on a high after yours went so well!" Bethany grinned at her.

"OK," Sara said slowly. Then she added, "But I was watching you in maths, Chloe, and you looked really unhappy."

"Er, *yes*, Sara." Chloe eyed her disbelievingly.

"You really were totally out of it for the first part of the lesson, weren't you? You had a pretty good excuse but I'd have thought Miss James could get through to anyone, no problem. Wow. She was really having a go at me."

"What are you talking about?" Sara frowned. Had she missed something?

"You remember what Miss James said about your maths homework a couple of weeks ago?"

Sara nodded and shuddered. She wasn't likely to forget.

"Mmm, exactly. Well, try doubling it and adding extra sarcasm. She was *not* a happy bunny."

"What did you do?" asked Sara in horror.

"The wrong exercises. And she said she wouldn't have minded so much if I'd got any of them right. I have to do both now *and* finish all that worksheet. So I think I'm allowed to look a bit down."

Sara looked embarrassed. "Sorry," she muttered.

Chloe smiled. "Don't worry. It's nice to know one less person heard me being yelled at. And you're allowed to be on cloud nine today!"

CHAPTER FOUR
The Big News

Sara didn't know quite what to say to her parents. She dawdled home from the bus stop, trying to work out the best way of putting it. It was so unfair! Any of her friends' parents would have been delighted with her news. Why did hers have to be so serious? Luckily, as she opened the front door, she heard her gran's voice in the kitchen and raced to find her. Here was one person who'd take the news properly!

"Gran! You'll never guess what!"

"What, love?" Her gran eyed her hopefully. She knew all about the audition, of course, and she knew that Sara had been expecting the callback list to go up today. She'd popped in on purpose.

"I got it! There were only five of us girls and I'm the only Year Seven. Isn't that brilliant?"

"Sara, what are you talking about?" Her mother was gazing worriedly at her over a mug of tea.

Sara turned a carefully blank face to her. She knew she was only at Shine because her gran had fought for her, and she'd pretty much given up trying to get her mother to take any interest in what happened at school, but it was really difficult not to mind. "The big audition I told you about was yesterday. I got a callback. For a second audition," she added, as her mother looked confused.

"Oh." Her mum's voice was thoughtful. "And you knew about this?" she asked Sara's gran.

"Of course I did!" Gran looked indignant and it was obvious that she was holding herself back from giving her daughter a talking to. "I thought Sara had told you about it, too," she added pointedly.

"I did," Sara agreed. "Last week. You *and* Dad." At least her mum had the grace to look slightly embarrassed, she thought.

"This is for the musical," her mum murmured slowly.

"*Mary Poppins*," Gran said in an irritated voice. "And it's a lead role. You've done so well, Sara, just getting this far. I'm really proud of you."

"So," her mother was using a 'getting my head round this' voice, "you've got a second audition for a large part in a musical…"

"Yes!" Sara was trying hard not to sound

irritated now as well. "I told you about all of this!"

"Mmm. Yes, sorry, Sara. I don't think I took it in."

Gran sniffed, as though she wasn't surprised, and she and Sara exchanged a meaningful glance. Then Sara looked back at her mother expectantly. Finally she was going to get some kind of praise – maybe even some excitement.

Her mum leaned across the table. "So how will this affect your school work?"

Sara gaped at her, absolutely speechless. Then she got up and raced upstairs to her room, not even hearing Gran start to tell Mum *exactly* what she thought of her.

Luckily at school the next day none of the others asked how her parents had taken the news, as Sara didn't think she could have told them without either bursting into tears or throwing something. (Preferably at her mother, but Lizabeth would have done as a substitute.) Her mum hadn't even said anything when she called her down for tea, although Sara did think she might have been crying, which wasn't like her at all.

Everyone doing the callback had extra lunchtime classes with Mr Lessing and Mr Harvey. Sara realized with horror that this meant she would have to be in the same room as Lizabeth. She might even be forced to *talk* to her. When it got to Wednesday lunchtime, she hung around with the others for as long as she possibly could.

"Aren't you meant to be at the studio in a minute?" Lily asked, checking her watch.

"Mmm," Sara replied gloomily.

"What's the matter?" said Chloe. "I'd have thought you'd have been desperate to get started."

"I would be, if it weren't for Lizabeth being there, too," Sara said crossly.

Lily stared at her. "But *you're* not scared of Lizabeth!" she said in surprise.

Sara shook her head. "No. But I'm going to be the only Year Seven there. I just get this feeling that she's not going to make it easy for me. I'm putting it off as long as I can, that's all. I had better go, though."

"Don't you dare go in looking like that," said Bethany sternly. "You know what Lizabeth's like. If she gets one sniff that you're worried, she'll be on you like a shark smelling blood."

Chloe laughed and Bethany glared at her. "You know it's true!" she said indignantly.

"Yes, but Lizabeth the shark! I can't help thinking of the shark from *Jaws* in a long blond wig."

That even made Sara giggle and Bethany

nodded approvingly. "Do – not –let – her – see – you – care – that – she – exists!" she added firmly, prodding a finger at Sara on each word. Then they frogmarched her to the studio and practically shoved her through the door.

Luckily Lizabeth and Nadia weren't there yet, but, unfortunately, neither was Mr Harvey. Sara shut the door behind her very slowly and trailed over to the small group by the piano. All the boys were there and the other two girls. She forced herself to look confident and was rewarded by a friendly smile from the tall girl with startlingly green eyes.

"Hi. I'm Amy. Are you Sara? Well, you must be because you're definitely not in our year! Congratulations! That's really amazing, getting a callback for something like this after you haven't even been here a month."

Sara flushed. "Yes – I mean, yes, I'm Sara! I think it was just luck though, honestly."

Amy nodded. "I know what you mean. I've done a few auditions now and the only time I got a part was the worst one I ever did! I totally messed up the lines they gave me to do and I was so embarrassed. This girl I once met at an audition for a cereal ad told me that most times they make a decision about eight seconds after you walk in the door. I *think* she was exaggerating but it makes you realize – sometimes whether you get the part or not isn't really anything to do with you."

Sara nodded. "Mmm… They've picked a lot of blond girls, haven't they? I think they want us to look like the girl from the film."

The other Year Eight girl twirled her long brown plait and grinned at Sara. "I'm planning on bleaching it before Monday! What with you, Amy and the one and only Lizabeth, it's too much of a coincidence. Even Nadia's almost blond."

Amy sniffed. "That's being generous. She's mouse."

Sara started to relax a bit. Amy and the brown-haired girl seemed really nice. She'd sort of assumed they would be like Lizabeth because they were Year Eight, but she realized now that was stupid.

"You won't really bleach your hair, will you?" she asked, a little shyly. "It's a lovely colour."

The brown-haired girl squinted down at the long ends of her plait. It *was* lovely, a rich chestnutty brown and slightly wavy. She shrugged. "No, I shouldn't think so. I kind of like it, and I'm not that desperate to be in this. Not *quite*, anyway."

"So, if you three reckon it's all done on looks, why did they choose us lot?" One of the boys was leaning against the piano grinning at them – he'd obviously been listening.

"You're all short!" the brown-haired girl threw back, smiling. "You're meant to be younger than us, remember."

"I'm not short!" He shot up from his relaxed pose against the piano, practically standing on tiptoe. "I'm way taller than you." Then he looked again at the brown-haired girl and shrugged. "Well, maybe not you, Izzy, but I'm definitely taller than her." He jerked a thumb at Sara. "Look. 'Scuse me a minute." He grabbed Sara's shoulders and moved her away from the piano. Then he stood back to back with her. "Loads taller."

Sara felt herself blushing again as the boy leaned against her. She didn't know whether she ought to complain about being moved around like some sort of doll, but she had no idea what to say, so she stayed quiet.

Amy and Izzy looked them up and down, measuring them, and exchanged grins. "Nah. Well, I don't know. What do you think, Iz?" Amy winked at Sara.

"Sorry, Nathan. Sara's taller – only by a whisker, mind…" Izzy was giggling.

Nathan's outraged face was so funny, Sara couldn't help joining in the teasing, even though five minutes ago she wouldn't have dared. "I've always thought the boy in the film was really weird-looking. A bit frog-like? Maybe that's what they're going for…" She put her head on one side thoughtfully, staring at Nathan, and Amy and Izzy nearly wet themselves laughing.

Nathan was speechless, and the rest of the boys were laughing, too. It was just then that Lizabeth and Nadia walked in, clearly hoping to make a grand entrance. Lizabeth was not happy about being upstaged and she stalked over to the giggling group.

"What on earth is the matter with you lot?" she asked contemptuously, arms folded.

Nathan recovered the power of speech

remarkably quickly. "We were having a joke, Lizabeth. Something you wouldn't understand, seeing as you don't actually have a sense of humour."

Sara grinned, then wished she hadn't when Lizabeth flashed her a furious glance. She was obviously about to lay into them when Mr Harvey walked in.

Mr Harvey was in his usual insulting mode. "Right, well, I have *absolutely* no idea why they chose you lot but obviously I will be doing my best with the very poor material on offer." He took the sting out of the words with a very small smile – more of a twitch, really, but everyone beamed back at him. "In their infinite wisdom, the casting team still wish to hear you sing 'A Spoonful of Sugar' – who knows why!"

Even Sara, who really loved the song, was getting the feeling that one could actually have too much sugar. But hey, it was for a good cause.

Mr Harvey made them sing bits of the song together, and then separately – he was really focusing on making sure the words were clear. The others all had good voices – even Lizabeth, Sara reluctantly had to admit. Her voice was very strong and she had superb control of her breathing, really holding on to the high notes.

At the end of the session, Sara walked out with Izzy and Amy, glad that she'd ended up meeting them. She cast a quick look back at Lizabeth and was startled to see a very thoughtful expression on her face. Then suddenly Lizabeth seemed to notice she was watching and she slapped on a sickly-sweet smile. Which was the scariest thing yet…

The others crowded round her when she got back to the classroom, just as Miss James was about to take registration.

"You're still alive, then," Bethany pointed out cheerfully.

Sara grinned. "Yeah, the other girls were really nice actually. And one of the boys."

"Whoo-oo!" Chloe whistled.

"Don't get excited, Chloe." Sara rolled her eyes at her friend. "Just because you fancy the pants off Sam, it doesn't mean the rest of us are boy-obsessed." She laughed – Chloe's face looked very like Nathan's when she'd made the frog comment. "I only liked him because he was rude to Lizabeth."

"She didn't have a go at you then?" Bethany asked, sounding relieved.

"No. Actually it was really weird, she gave me this totally fake smile as I was going. I didn't know what to make of it."

"She's probably trying to psych you out," Lily suggested bitterly. "So was the class any good?"

Sara gave them a quick rundown of what they'd done and then they had to shoot off to singing.

"More Mr Harvey!" Sara shook her head. "Please, please don't let him do 'A Spoonful of Sugar'…"

Lizabeth carried on being weird. At break on Thursday, Bethany nudged Sara. "You know what you said about you-know-who smiling at you? She's at it again. Look!"

Sure enough, Lizabeth was walking past with Nadia, both smiling sweet, friendly smiles at Sara and Bethany. They seemed to have been practising, as the smiles looked almost natural.

"That was truly weird," Bethany
pronounced as soon as they'd gone round the
corner. "We need to keep an eye on those two."

"They *could* just have been smiling." Sara
said, not sounding very convinced.

"Yeah, right…"

But it seemed Sara was right. At lunch,
Lizabeth wafted past their table, smiled as
though Sara was her favourite person in the
world – and then turned back as though she'd
just thought of something. Her blue eyes were

enormous as she leaned over to talk to Sara. Everyone else at the table watched in amazement as Lizabeth cooed, "Sara! I'm really sorry, I've been meaning to say this for ages." She swept her long dark eyelashes artistically down and up again. "I shouldn't have said what I did after the first audition. It was just —" she flapped her hand vaguely – "the stress. The buzz of the audition really got to me. You know? Anyway, I'm really sorry. See you later for coaching!" And she went, leaving them all sitting in stunned silence.

"I do not believe it…" Chloe muttered. "Lizabeth Mackenzie just apologized to you, Sara. Wow. Do you think the cafeteria has security cameras? We need this for posterity."

"I don't trust her an inch." Bethany was frowning. "She didn't mean one word of that."

Lily nodded. "I felt like making the sign of the cross, like they do in vampire films. That girl is so evil."

Sara agreed with her. But then – were they being unfair? *She'd* felt really weird about the audition, too. She'd been worrying about competing with her mates, desperate to impress her parents and, above all, just determined to do well. Adrenaline could do funny things to a person and she'd often felt buzzed or down after the excitement of a performance. She still didn't actually *like* Lizabeth, of course, but surely it wasn't really that strange for her to have had a temper tantrum like that after something so important.

"I don't know..." she muttered thoughtfully.

"You weren't convinced by that little act, were you?" Bethany looked shocked. "Sara, you just can't be that *nice*!" She said *nice* as though she meant *stupid*.

"I'm just saying maybe!" Sara said defensively. "You never know, I suppose."

"Yes, we do." Chloe leaned over the table and glared at Sara. "Lizabeth is awful. Don't trust her!"

CHAPTER FIVE
Lizabeth's True Colours

Despite Chloe's warning, Sara was finding it hard to hate her as much as usual. Maybe it was the glory of being the only person Lizabeth had ever been known to apologize to, or perhaps it was just that Sara knew Lizabeth was going through the same stress as she was.

"Well, what am I supposed to do?" she asked her friends before school on Monday. Lizabeth had just walked past them and called out, "Good luck for later, Sara!", and Sara had rather feebly called back, "Yeah, good luck to you, too…" Then she'd seen Chloe, Lily and Bethany gazing at her reproachfully. "Don't look at me like I just kicked a puppy or something! What do you want me to do, ignore her? How can I when she's being nice?"

"Trust us, she is *never* nice," Bethany muttered darkly. "She's plotting. She has to be."

"That's what Amy and Izzy said on Friday when she was being all sweet to me at our coaching session," Sara admitted. "They don't like her either, even though she's in their class."

"You see!" Bethany said triumphantly. "Everyone in the school knows she's a monster, apart from you! Just remember what she was like to Lily!"

Sara nibbled her nails. "But she *was* being really nice, Bethany. She was paired up with me in one of the improvisations we did and she seemed – oh, I don't know … normal.

She was telling me how excited she was and she loves the film of *Mary Poppins* just as much as I do. She told me all this interesting stuff she'd found online about the filming. And she gave me some good audition tips! She explained centring yourself way better than when Mr Lessing tried to teach us it."

The others were still looking at her sceptically and Sara sighed. "Oh, you're probably right. I just can't think straight today. I can't believe it's Monday already. The audition's this afternoon!"

"Stop doing that to your nails!" Lily grabbed her hand away. "Do you want to have ratty nails for the casting team to see?"

"They aren't going to be looking at her hands, Lils!" Chloe giggled.

"You never know," said Lily seriously. "Casting directors can have pet hates like everybody else. What if one of them just can't stand seeing people with bitten nails?"

Sara stared down at her fingers in horror. She'd only bitten one nail a little way round. Was it enough to lose her the part?

"Look what you've done!" Bethany sighed. "Sara, Lily was just saying. This casting team probably couldn't care less about your nails."

"You think?" Sara was still staring anxiously at her fingers.

Everything seemed to be significant today. Breakfast with her family had been a nightmare. Sara had really hoped that her parents might make a bit of a fuss of her on such an important day, but Mum had been going on and on about some school thing that she had to organize. Will had wished her good luck as she got up to go and catch her bus, and she was fairly sure that she'd heard her dad asking him why. Mum definitely knew the audition was happening – she couldn't have forgotten after that row with Gran – but she just hadn't bothered to say anything.

Sitting in registration, Sara kept patting her pocket to make sure the little cat was still there. She'd gone round to Gran's house on Sunday, nervous and desperate to talk to someone about the audition. They were sitting in the kitchen chatting when suddenly Gran had handed her a tiny parcel wrapped up with ribbon.

"What is it?" Sara asked.

Gran smiled mysteriously. "Open it."

Sara had carefully undone the wrapping and picked out the little black felt cat. He was sitting with his tail curled round his legs and he had green sequins for eyes, a pink bead nose and thread whiskers. He looked really old. He *was* really old, Sara knew that. She'd seen him sitting on Gran's dressing table ever since she could remember.

"It's Jacky! Gran, why've you given me Jacky?" Sara gazed down at the little creature in her hand, feeling confused.

Gran smiled. "I bought him just before my first professional audition, Sara. Tomorrow's your first audition for a part, so I thought you might like to have him as your mascot now."

"Do you mean it? Oh, Gran!" Sara couldn't stop her eyes filling with tears. Gran couldn't have done anything to make her feel more special.

Sara felt herself blinking back tears now as she touched the little cat in her pocket. She still couldn't believe Gran had given Jacky to her. She'd kept him for over sixty years. Sara hadn't shown him to the others yet. He was so special and for the moment she just wanted him to be a secret between her and Gran. Jacky seemed to be helping her a little already. It was comforting just to be able to slip her hand into her pocket and remember that Gran thought she deserved to have him.

Suddenly Lily nudged her and Sara blinked in confusion.

"She's here, Miss James!" Bethany said and Sara blushed, realizing that she'd missed her name being called.

Miss James didn't seem to mind, though. She smiled at Sara and said, "It's the audition today, isn't it? Ms Purcell mentioned that you'd have to leave maths early. Don't worry, I'm sure you'll catch up."

Sara exchanged grins with the others. As if missing something vital in the maths lesson was what she was worried about!

It was a good thing she wasn't worried because she took in precisely nothing from any of her morning classes. She just couldn't stop the words from the song running through her head, and Bethany and the others had to keep shooing her in the right direction when it came to change rooms at the end of geography. She wouldn't have had any of the right books either, if they hadn't actually packed her rucksack for her.

By the time it got to maths, she was one big ball of jittery excitement. Luckily Miss James seemed to have realized there wasn't much point expecting her to say anything useful.

"What time do you have to go?" Lily whispered when the maths teacher was talking to someone else.

"Twelve," Sara muttered. The clock seemed to be moving far faster than it ought to be, she was sure. "The audition's at half past, but I have to change and everything… Mr Harvey said to go at twelve. I'm the last of the girls. It's Nadia, then Izzy, then Lizabeth, then Amy, then me. And then they're doing the boys."

At one minute to twelve, Sara waved a shaky arm in the air. Miss James looked a bit surprised as she'd just asked a difficult question and Sara was by no means a star at maths. Then she remembered. "Oh, yes, you need to go, don't you? Well good luck, Sara. Don't forget to get the homework off one of the others."

Sara nodded vaguely and the rest of the class waved and grinned at her, calling good luck messages as she slowly headed for the door. Her legs were trembling. She was going to have to sing, dance and probably go through a scene in about half an hour – at the moment she could hardly walk! Let's just concentrate on getting changed first, she decided.

Izzy was in the changing room, looking relieved.

"Have you had your audition? How was it?" Sara gasped out. "Were they nice? Was it the same people? What did you have to do?"

Izzy grinned. "Slow down, slow down! Yeah, they were really nice. It was Tamara, the choreographer from last time, and that musical director, Simon. The director was there, too, which was a bit scary but he was OK."

Sara nodded. Good. She'd liked Simon and Tamara. "So what did you have to do?"

"You start getting changed and I'll tell you,"

Izzy said firmly. "You've not got time to stand around."

Sara couldn't help giggling. Izzy reminded her of Bethany, with that slightly bossy looking-after-you tone of voice. She grabbed her footless tights and Shine T-shirt out of her locker.

"Don't forget to brush your hair out," Izzy said. "They want it down, remember."

"Oh, yeah, I forgot. Yours looks fab down!"

Izzy's chestnut-brown hair was in a great cloud all around her shoulders. She grimaced. "It looks nice but it was a nightmare doing the dancing. I had to keep shaking it back and it put my timing off. You'd better watch that. But yours is nice and straight, so it won't be as much of a problem." She grabbed a brush and started to fight the wavy mass back into its plait.

"So go on then, what happened?" Sara

prompted Izzy.

"It was pretty much like last time, except they gave me a scene from the musical to do. One of the casting team read in Michael and I was Jane. I had to do it about three times. It was just like Mr Lessing said – trying to do what they ask each time. It was tricky though. You can't help feeling like you did it wrong the last time when they ask you to change something."

Sara chewed her lip thoughtfully. That did sound hard but then they did that sort of thing with Mr Lessing all the time. Perhaps she could just try and think of it like a class, instead of an audition. At least talking to Izzy had made her feel a bit more normal. She glanced at her watch.

"Eeeek! I'd better go. Thanks, Izzy. See you later!"

"Break a leg!" Izzy called after her as she

dashed out of the door. "Hey, I didn't mean it! Slow down!" Izzy was right – falling down the stairs on the way to the audition would just be totally stupid, so Sara forced herself to walk sensibly.

She was coming along the corridor that led to the small studio when she met Lizabeth coming the other way. The older girl gave her a relieved smile.

"Oh, Sara!" Lizabeth squeaked. "Oh, I'm so glad I caught you. I've just had my audition – I was so nervous! And it was really awful, the piano was out of tune. Simon – you know, the one who did the singing audition last time? He said it had been getting worse all morning. So in the middle of my audition we had to move studios! I completely lost the mood, it was really unfair. But anyway, they're doing Amy's audition now and they sent me to tell you to go and wait outside the south studio instead, OK? Then when Amy comes out she'll tell you if they want you to go straight in or if someone's going to come and fetch you."

Sara nodded, a little bewildered by Lizabeth rattling on. She seemed to be nervous, too. It was obviously the stress from her nightmare audition. Thank goodness it hadn't been *her* slot when the piano went wrong!

"It must have been awful," she said sympathetically, feeling really sorry for Lizabeth.

"It was," Lizabeth shuddered dramatically. She seemed to have calmed down a bit now. "I could tell something was wrong, but it was only just slightly off, you know? I thought it was me. And even when we started again I just couldn't get back on track. Oh well." She sighed. "You know where the south studio is, don't you?"

"I *think* so..." Sara said slowly. She wasn't quite sure which one it was. Because the school was an old building, it had practice rooms and studios scattered all over the place.

Lizabeth pointed. "You go back up the corridor, past the cafeteria and down that little flight of stairs and then you just keep turning left – it says south studio on the door. Anyway, I'd better go and change. Hope yours goes well! You were really good in the coaching session on Friday. Don't forget to centre yourself before you start the scene!" And she smiled and raced off, leaving Sara still gazing after her.

Sara wished Lizabeth had stopped long enough to show her exactly where the new studio was, but she was already gone. Still, if it had the name on the door it couldn't be too hard to find.

She checked her watch – still only twenty past twelve. She had plenty of time really, but she wanted to find the studio and have time to gather herself together a bit. She was feeling all over the place.

She turned back and trotted off, following Lizabeth's directions. After what seemed like an age, she turned a corner and saw the big soundproofed door, with the sign on it – *South Studio*.

There were a couple of chairs outside and Sara sank on to one gratefully. She'd do some warm-up exercises in a minute but now she just needed to calm down.

Sara dug her nails into the palms of her hands, trying desperately to focus. The unexpected encounter with Lizabeth had thrown her. She'd visualized the audition happening in the small studio (a tip from Mr Lessing), and the change of venue was a shock. Sara tried to take deep, slow breaths, but her nerves had come back full force and she found herself gulping great mouthfuls of air. "In – one, two, three. Out – one, two, three," she muttered to herself crossly. It was stupid to be so nervous!

Sara forced herself to think about what Gran had said yesterday, "If they've called you back for a second audition, it means they like you! Don't think of it as a test or something horrible that you've got to get through. It's a good thing – they've done you a favour and you want them to like you even more. So be yourself and be nice!" Then she'd smiled a funny little smile and added, "Though if you need to be horrible, dear, don't hesitate…"

Sara had given her a surprised look and Gran laughed. "There were a lot of girls going after not a lot of parts when I was starting out, Sara. I'm not saying I resorted to any dirty tricks, but I saw a lot done and I suffered a couple of times. It makes you a lot less sympathetic, I can tell you. Sometimes you have to be ruthless..." She went on to tell Sara all sorts of stories about understudies doing awful things like greasing stairs to knock out the principal and get a chance to go on stage.

Sara was still feeling horribly hollow inside but thinking of Gran helped a bit. She checked her watch. It was twelve twenty-nine! She looked worriedly at the studio door. Shouldn't Amy have come out by now? Mr Lessing had said they'd probably want five minutes' discussion time between each audition. Sara guessed they were running late, probably because they'd had to swap studios.

Thinking about it, it was weird about that piano going out of tune. The school was really careful about that kind of thing. They had to be...

Sara wandered up and down the corridor, trying to breathe calmly and think of the song lyrics and all the advice anyone had ever given her, but she just kept coming back to Lizabeth. She'd been really jumpy and nervous at first – quite strange. Not like herself at all. She hadn't even been like that after the first audition, when she'd said the adrenaline made her so angry with Sara. So what was it that had made her act so oddly?

Was it that she'd been pulling a trick, like the ones Gran had described? She'd suddenly seemed much calmer when Sara had been sympathetic. When Sara had believed her… Sara looked back at the studio door. She didn't dare open it. If Lizabeth had been telling the truth, she'd interrupt Amy's audition. But what if Amy's audition had actually just finished – on the other side of the school?

CHAPTER SIX
Race Against Time

Suddenly Sara heard footsteps pounding towards her and she tensed up. What was going on? Was it Lizabeth coming back? Then Nathan raced round the corner and dashed up to her. He grabbed her hand and dragged her along as she protested, "Hey! What's going on?!"

"You've been stitched up, Sara!" he panted. "Lizabeth! Come on! I'll explain on the way but we haven't got much time. Amy'll be done any minute." Sara pelted after him, furious with herself. The others had been right all along – Lizabeth's niceness *had* all been a trick. She had let herself be taken in, even after all those stories from Gran!

"I can't believe I was so stupid!" she moaned as she followed Nathan down the corridor. "She told me the piano had gone out of tune and they'd changed studios! I'm going to miss my audition!"

"Not if we really run." Nathan picked up speed, weaving around everyone else in the corridors. "They were way behind time. Amy hadn't even gone in when I got there. And don't feel bad about it. Lizabeth's really sneaky. We've all had a year to get to know how low she can go and I was still shocked. I was just starting to wonder where you'd got to when I saw her pop her head back round the corner with this evil smirk on her face. She was checking if you were there, in case you hadn't believed her. Nadia was with her as well. Toby and me heard them whispering. Lizabeth was going on about how clever she was, and how they'd think you'd got stage fright and you weren't professional."

"So you came to get me!" Sara panted.

"There was no way I was letting her get away with it. Here we are." They screeched to a stop outside the small studio. Toby was waiting for them anxiously.

"You found her! Well done, mate! I reckon you're just in time, Sara. You're so lucky they're overrunning. Amy's still in there. You've not got long though – it's twelve forty! I was worried they might be going really fast so I came along as soon as lunch started." He looked a bit embarrassed admitting to this. "Then we saw that little monster Lizabeth plotting and Nathan raced off for you. I was going to try and stall them if Amy finished." He sounded very relieved that he wasn't going to have to. "Here, do you want some water?" He tugged a bottle out of his bag and offered it to Sara, who gulped it down gratefully. Then she went over to the window and peered at her reflection in the glass.

"Oh no! I look like a beetroot!" She ran her fingers through her hair desperately. How could she audition when she was out of breath, bright red, sweaty and her hair looked like a bird's nest?

Looking even more embarrassed, Toby produced a comb and Sara quickly raked it through her hair. "I don't suppose you've got some powder as well?" she asked, giggling a bit hysterically.

"Stop talking and just breathe," Nathan said. "Amy'll be done any minute, and they're bound to do the singing first, that would be just our luck."

Sara nodded, perched herself on the windowsill and tried to slow down her racing heartbeat. And then the door opened.

Amy came out looking exhausted and gave her a small grin. "Hiya. They want you to go straight in because they're so behind time. Hope it goes well!"

Sara nodded and got up. She went to open the door, then suddenly turned back and gave Nathan a massive hug, ignoring Amy's shocked face. "Thank you!" she squeaked, turning bright red again. Then she took a deep breath and pulled the door open.

Sara was so relieved to actually be at the audition, and not in the wrong place entirely, that she couldn't really feel nervous. Not as badly nervous as she had been waiting outside the south studio, anyway. She smiled brightly at everyone as she closed the door, then felt a bit silly. Maybe she should have been a bit more formal? But luckily, the three people in the room were smiling back.

"So you must be Sara," said the tall dark-haired man, looking down at his notes. "I'm Jasper, I'm the director. And you've already met Tamara and Simon." He grinned at her. "Are you nervous?"

It was such an unexpected question that Sara answered without even thinking about it. "A little…" she agreed shyly. Then she was horrified. Surely she wasn't supposed to say yes! She was supposed to be totally calm and professional and—

"Don't panic!" He was still grinning. "Anyone who isn't nervous at an audition is an idiot as far as I'm concerned. A good dose of nerves really helps, anyway."

Sara nodded, feeling relieved, but she was still a bit overawed. She hadn't really taken it in when Izzy said that the director was here – the director of the whole show, just to watch her! But then the children were on stage almost all the time in *Mary Poppins* – and Mary Poppins was their nanny, so she wouldn't even be there if the children weren't. So they were pretty important parts really… It was the nerves making the thoughts whirl round her head. Sara gulped and wished they could just get on with it.

"So." Jasper was walking round her now, looking her up and down, and Sara couldn't help turning her head to follow him round. What was he *doing*? Were her ankles actually that important? "Simon was very impressed with your voice last time, Sara. I have to say, I've heard 'A Spoonful of Sugar' rather too many times this morning—"

"I know what you mean," Sara put in helpfully. "It gets a bit much, doesn't it?" Then she went scarlet. *Shut up, shut up, shut up!* She was so nervous it was making her ditzy. Simon was laughing at her. She was so messing this up!

"Glad you agree," Jasper said, his grin even wider. "So let's have something else. Do you know any other songs from the show?"

Sara nodded, her mouth firmly closed.

She was determined not to say anything else stupid.

"Such as?" Simon prompted hopefully, and Sara felt like sinking into the floor.

"I really like 'Feed the Birds'," she admitted in an embarrassed whisper. "But the children don't sing that, do they?"

"Doesn't matter." Simon sat down at the piano and riffled through the music. "Do you need the music to read from or are you better without?"

"Better without," said Sara firmly, pulling herself together. She just hoped that what he was going to play was like the film version because she'd never been properly taught the song. She only knew it from singing along with Julie Andrews!

Luckily the introduction seemed pretty familiar. Sara couldn't help thinking what Mr Harvey would say if he knew what she was about to do. He'd probably have a heart attack. All at once, the funny side of all this struck her and she couldn't help breaking into a huge smile. Simon was one of those impressive people who could play the piano without sheet music *and* without looking at what he was doing. He smiled back.

"Don't worry if you get lost, I'll help you out. And you come in after three. One, two, three…"

Sara loved this song. It always made her cry, however often she watched the film. Julie Andrews's voice was so beautiful and the words were so sad. She forgot about how stupid she'd been and just enjoyed herself.

Simon was such a good accompanist, she could tell he was following her rather than the other way around and it made it so easy. She felt like hugging him when she finished but had just enough sense to realize she probably wasn't supposed to hug people in an audition. But she couldn't not say thank you.

"You played it perfectly," she breathed. "I've never sung it like that before."

Jasper was scribbling furiously in his notes. "That was great. I'd ask you to dance to it but it isn't really a dancing sort of song. It's one of the few pieces in the show that's quite still. Let's see how we do with a scene and we'll move on to dancing at the end."

The scene was an argument between Jane and Michael Banks and it was really funny. Though it was funnier still trying to pretend

Jasper was her little brother! After what Izzy had said earlier, Sara was prepared to be told to change things around and she did her best to follow the directions without being fazed. After all, it was what actors had to do, even the most famous ones. At least Jasper seemed to be fairly happy, getting her to try the scene a few times in different ways.

Eventually, he said, "Lovely. Right. What's the time? Oh, wow, we're so behind. Tamara, you were happy with Sara's dancing, weren't you? Do you need to see any more?"

Tamara looked thoughtful. "No, I think we're fine. We really do need to get on with the boys." She smiled at Sara. "You were very capable last week."

Sara wasn't sure whether to feel pleased or not. Was it good that they didn't need to see her dance? Or did it mean that they definitely didn't want her and just didn't want to waste time?

"Thank you very much, Sara." Jasper had his head buried in his notes again. "Can you ask, umm, Nathan, to come in please?"

Sara nodded. Now the audition was over, she could see why Amy had looked so exhausted. It felt like she'd done a ten-mile run and she hadn't even had to dance! She just about remembered that she was still on show as she thanked them and went to the door – she felt like keeling over.

Outside, she managed to grin at Nathan and tell him to go in. Then she flopped on to the windowsill and made a 'thank goodness that's over' face at Toby, who was sitting in the corner of the window looking terrified.

"What were they like?" he asked anxiously. "Were you OK? Could you sing all right?"

Sara nodded thoughtfully, trying to think back over the audition. "They were nice. I *think* the singing was OK. The director said he was sick of 'A Spoonful of Sugar' and he got me to sing 'Feed the Birds' instead."

Toby looked horrified. "Whaaat? Oh no, I'm toast then!"

"It's all right, he'll have had a rest from it by the time you go in. Anyway, you must know loads of other songs. I bet that Simon could play anything. I wouldn't worry about it." Sara patted him on the back encouragingly. "Have you been sitting here all this time? You'd better get up and move around or you'll be all stiff."

Although she was still shattered, Sara was starting to relax, the tension of the audition easing out of her. Suddenly she desperately wanted to go and find her friends. She needed Chloe to tell her a stupid joke or something.

"I'd better go and get something to eat before I collapse," she told Toby. "Best of luck – and thanks for the comb and the water. You and Nathan saved my life! See you later!"

⭐⭐⭐

The cafeteria was full, and Sara couldn't see Bethany, Chloe and Lily until they bounced up next to her and dragged her to a table.

"What was it like? Tell us everything!" Chloe commanded.

Sara looked around at them all. "You were right," she admitted. "Lizabeth was plotting. You'll never believe what she did." She explained about Lizabeth's sneaky trick and how Nathan had rescued her. The others listened in horror.

"Anyway," Sara finished. "I'm really, really sorry. I should have listened to you more. I can't believe she nearly got away with it."

"Are you going to tell someone?" Lily asked.

Sara shrugged. "I don't know. What would I say? I'd look so stupid. And actually, I have to say, she did me a favour—"

"How come?" Bethany sounded disbelieving.

"I was so nervous this morning. I mean, really, really nervous."

"Well, you seemed a bit out of it," Chloe agreed, "but you weren't that bad, were you? You looked OK."

"Chloe, I'd practically forgotten how to walk, let alone sing and dance. But I was so relieved to get to the audition in one piece that I almost forgot all of that. I was still a bit nervous but *nothing* like before. I'm sure I did better than I would have if I'd been on time and waiting outside for ages. Toby – he's one of the boys auditioning – he was there for ages and he looked so scared. I hope he's OK." Sara checked her watch. "He's probably about to go in now."

"Look," Chloe hissed. "Lizabeth. What are we going to do? We have to do *something*!"

Lizabeth was walking through the crowded cafeteria, looking curiously at Sara. "So, how was your audition?" she asked in a sarcastic tone as she reached their table, obviously expecting Sara to burst into tears.

"Fine, thank you," Sara purred. "I really enjoyed it. We'll just have to see what happens now, won't we? Best of luck, Lizabeth." She smiled back sweetly, mimicking Lizabeth, and watched the older girl's face change, the smile faltering to a confused frown as she tried to work out what was going on.

Lizabeth looked round quickly at Chloe, Bethany and Lily, all glaring at her, and for once her confidence seemed to break. She backed away and disappeared out of the cafeteria.

"She's probably thinking that even if she gets the part, you'll tell and it'll be taken away from her," Bethany said happily. "That was the best revenge, Sara. She hasn't a clue what to do now."

"Let's hope it lasts a while!" said Lily. "Now tell us what it was like!"

Sara tried to remember every little detail, and they discussed the possibilities eagerly till the end of lunch. No one could work out whether not having to dance was good or bad, and they were still arguing about it as they changed for tap.

Ms Driver was just as keen to hear about the audition, and she called Sara over when they came in. She said that sometimes it was impossible to tell how auditions had really gone. "But you did dance very well last week, Sara," she said, smiling. "You really pulled out all the stops. That's a very important quality – being able to perform when you need to."

Sara blushed delightedly. Now that the audition was over, she was trying very hard to let go and not stress about it. If she didn't get the part, it wouldn't be a disaster. The disaster would be if Lizabeth got it. If that happened, Sara just didn't know what she would do.

She had to debrief for Mr Harvey in singing, too, but he wasn't as horrified to hear about her singing 'Feed the Birds' as she'd expected. In fact, he made her sing it again for him! Then he totally picked it to pieces. If it hadn't been for Bethany murmuring, "Ignore him! Ignore him! You know what he's like!" in her ear, Sara might have decided she'd never be asked to audition for anything else ever again.

Mr Harvey was just explaining exactly what Sara had done so terribly wrong in the last verse, when the door opened and a rather nervous-looking girl edged round it. She looked as if she really didn't want to be there and everyone felt for her. Mr Harvey hated being interrupted.

"What?" he barked.

"Please-could-Sara-Sinclair-go-to-the-small-studio?" she rattled off hurriedly, obviously desperate to get away before he had a go at her.

Sara was completely shocked. They wanted her back? *Now?* Had they decided they wanted to see her dance after all? She wasn't in her dance clothes! With a worried look she turned to Mr Harvey, and discovered that, amazingly, he was beaming at her.

"Perhaps you didn't sing it quite that badly after all!" he said. "Or, of course, they could just be imbeciles who are completely lacking in taste. Off you go!"

Bethany hugged her and pushed her towards the door. "Hurry up!"

Sara found herself at the door of the studio before she knew quite how she'd got there. She knocked very, very quietly. Nothing happened. It was just going through her mind that this was some other awful trick of Lizabeth's when Nathan came round the corner, looking as confused as she felt.

"Sara! Did you get called out of class, too?"

"Yes. Do you think we're supposed to go in? I've knocked, but…" Sara stared at the door helplessly and then jumped out of her skin as it opened.

"Aha!" It was Jasper. "Excellent. Sara and Nathan. Thought I could hear voices. Come on in."

They followed him, exchanging excited glances. Tamara and Simon were still there, too, looking rather tired. Tamara was eating a sandwich and she waved it at them cheerfully.

"Now, sorry to drag you back again, but we just wanted to see you both together. Have you acted together before at all?" Jasper handed them scripts.

"N-no," Sara stammered. "Not really. We aren't in the same year."

"We did some improvisation as a pair when we had a class to prepare for the audition," Nathan put in.

"It doesn't matter. Can you read that same scene for me again? Try and remember the direction I gave you this morning and see if you can hit it off. Brother and sister, remember." He grinned at them and sat down in an 'I'm the audience, impress me' sort of way.

Nathan had the first line, thank goodness. Sara wasn't sure where her voice had actually gone – it certainly didn't seem to be where it should be. She looked at him hopefully. Could they pull this off?

Nathan took a deep breath, then a wicked glint came into his eye. He brandished his script under Sara's nose angrily and started their argument. Somehow, it wasn't difficult to spit her line back at him. He was such a brat!

On cue, Sara's voice miraculously came back and she gave as good as she got, trying hard to put in all the gestures and movements Jasper had suggested earlier on. Nathan was really fun to act with and very good at picking up on her tone of voice. The scene was supposed to finish with Jane throwing a doll at Michael and it seemed quite natural to hurl her script at him. He actually managed to catch it and stick his tongue out at her. They stood there feeling a bit lost after that and it was a relief when Jasper started to clap.

"Excellent. Very nice indeed." He looked over at Simon and Tamara questioningly and they both nodded. "Good. We just wanted to see you together. Obviously the relationship between Jane and Michael is very important."

Nathan and Sara nodded breathlessly. Did that mean…?

"So, dependent on contracts and all that sort of thing, we'd like to offer you two the parts.

142

We're going to have two casts for the children because we can't have you working every night, but you two will work together. OK?"

They nodded, speechless.

"All the arrangements will be made through the school," Jasper continued, "so your parents will get a letter in a couple of days. Congratulations! It's going to be fun working together. That last scene was great." And he came over and shook hands with them both. "You'd better get back to your classes. I was at school here, you know, a long, long time ago, and I remember how hard they make you work!"

"Thank you!" Sara stammered, and she and Nathan dashed out of the studio.

"We did it!" he yelped as soon as the door had shut. Then he hugged her.

Sara was jumping up and down and hugging him back at the same time. "We're going to be in *Mary Poppins!*"

Sara had done it. She had her first part. Gran would be so proud of her – and Jacky had brought her luck! Surely her parents would have to understand that Sara really should be at Shine after this. How many girls got a chance to be in a West End musical when they'd only had three weeks at stage school? They had to be impressed!

Sara and Nathan danced up and down the corridor, and as he hugged her again, Sara realized that spending lots more time with her co-star was going to make the whole thing even better…

Read an extract from

LILY'S SECRET AUDITION

CHAPTER ONE
Like Mother, Like Daughter?

Lily Ferrars raced into school, looking forward to meeting up with her mates. She hadn't seen them for a whole sixteen hours after all – chatting to Chloe on WhatsApp last night definitely didn't count. She galloped up the stairs to the Year Seven form room, grinning to herself. It seemed so weird that she'd fought against going to this school for ages and now she was desperate to get here!

Lily had planned to hate being at Shine

and to spend this year of exile not talking to anyone, but it hadn't quite worked out that way. She hadn't bargained on making three fantastic new friends in the first few weeks, and the atmosphere of the school was difficult to resist.

"Lily!" Sara bounded up behind her, with her face glowing, and Lily felt a teensy stab of jealousy. Sara had found out the day before that she'd got a part in a special Christmas run of *Mary Poppins* at a West End theatre. There was no doubt that Sara deserved to be at a stage school. Just looking at her now, star quality simply oozed out of her. Sara gave Lily a hug and the jealousy disappeared – Lily couldn't be anything but happy for such a good friend.

"Don't need to ask how you're feeling today!" she giggled. "Did you sleep at all last night?"

"Not much." Sara grinned. "It's so exciting. I can't wait for the letter to come from the theatre. Then it'll all be official. Contracts and everything."

They strolled into their classroom and loads of people called out their congratulations to Sara, who blushed, but grinned even wider. Chloe and Bethany were sitting on the windowsill the four of them had claimed as their own.

"Yay, Sara!" Chloe called. "Sing 'A Spoonful of Sugar'. I want to hear how the professionals do it!"

Sara dumped her bag and scrambled up next to them, making a face. "That's the one bad thing about this part – I've sung that song so many times. It used to be one of my favourites, but now I have to make it look as though I've never heard it before. On stage! Every day for weeks!"

"My mum said –" Lily started and then stopped, feeling embarrassed. Who wanted to hear what her mum said? But it seemed like the others did – they were all looking at her eagerly. Lily's mum was an actress, not a really famous one, but the kind that everyone recognizes from somewhere. Marina Ferrars was always on TV and she was hardly ever not working. Lily's dad was a lawyer who worked mostly with people in show business, so the Ferrars' house was always full of actor-types – what Lily's grandad always called 'luvvies'. Lily hated it. Or she always had done, anyway. Her mum was certain that Lily was going to be an actress as well and so she'd started her in dance classes at two and a half, drama at three and singing at four. At first Lily had loved it, especially the acting, but for the last few years it hadn't been that much fun.

"You're so lucky having a mum who knows

about all this stuff. What were you going to say?" Sara asked hopefully.

"Well, just that she was doing this play years ago, before I was born, and it was a really long run, so she knew the play backwards. One night she was tired – I think she'd been to a party or something the night before – and she suddenly realized she was on stage in the middle of the second act, and she had absolutely no idea how she'd got there. She couldn't remember saying any of the lines, what she'd done in the interval, anything."

"What happened? Was she OK?" Chloe asked. The others were all leaning in, half-excited, half-terrified.

"She was so scared she froze up, but she was in the middle of a scene with the guy who was playing her husband, and he sort of twisted some of the lines around so she could get back in without it being really obvious. She bought him a massive bar of chocolate the next day, she was so grateful."

"Wow." Sara shuddered. "I hope that doesn't happen to me."

"It won't," Lily said comfortingly. "She'd been doing that part for months. *Mary Poppins* isn't that long a run, is it? And you're alternating casts for the children. That's really good – you won't have a chance to get stale."

Bethany shook her head. "You know more about this stuff than anybody, Lily. You should set up an advice line for our year."

Lily flushed, wishing she'd never mentioned it. "Don't be silly," she said lightly. "I've never even had an audition." It wasn't exactly true, but then that was one of Lily's deepest, darkest secrets. "What about Chloe? You've had loads of work."

Chloe shook her head. "A whole lot of modelling and adverts and one tiny part in a

TV series. I don't know anything about theatre stuff."

Lily shrugged. "Well, I only know gossip from my mum and I'm sure she makes half of it up. In a few weeks' time Sara will be our theatre expert anyway!"

Lily felt a bit of a fraud when the others treated her like some sort of guru because of her mum. She hadn't even wanted to come to stage school! In Lily's last year at her smart primary school, her mum had brought home the prospectus for The Shine School for the Performing Arts. Everyone at her dance class was really jealous but Lily was furious. She wanted to go on to the same school as all her friends, not spend the next five years training for a job she was never going to do.

Coming Soon!

HOLLY WEBB

Holly Webb started out as a children's
book editor and wrote her first series for
the publisher she worked for. She has been
writing ever since, with over one hundred
books to her name. Holly lives in Berkshire,
with her husband and three children.
Holly's pet cats are always nosying around
when she is trying to type on her laptop.

For more information
about Holly Webb visit:

www.holly-webb.com